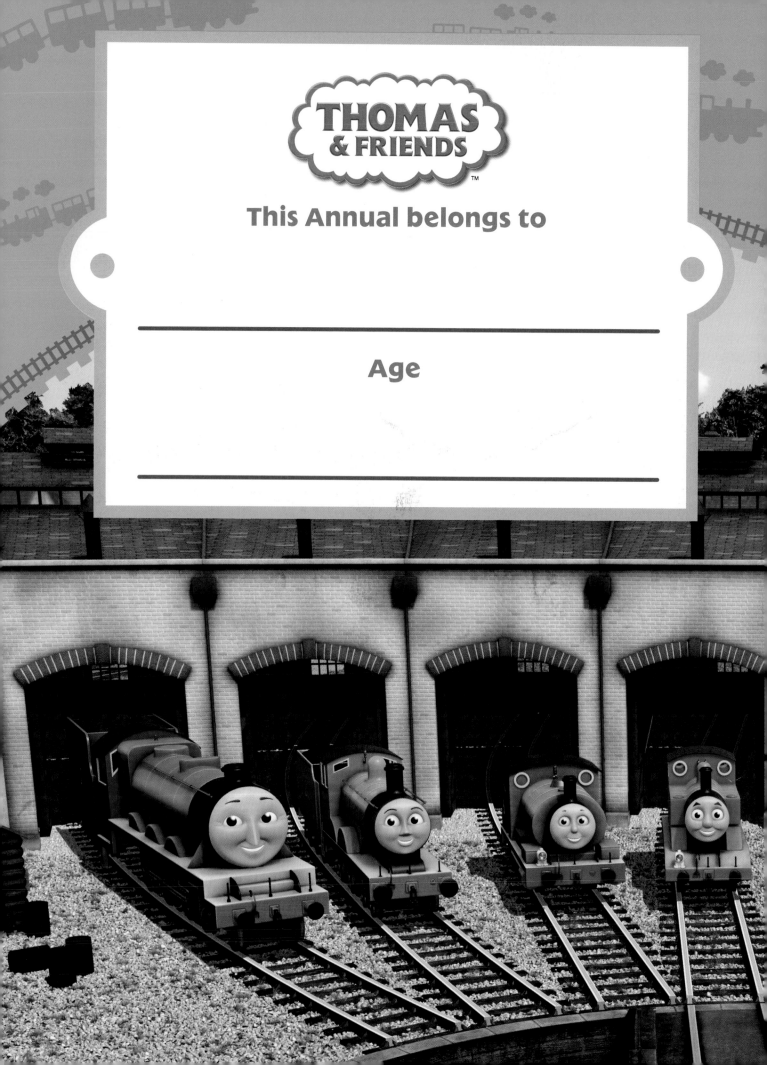

THOMAS & FRIENDS™

This Annual belongs to

Age

Contents

EGMONT
We bring stories to life

First published in Great Britain 2012 by Egmont UK Limited
239 Kensington High Street, London W8 6SA
Edited by Catherine Shoolbred.
Designed by Elaine Wilkinson and Claire Yeo.

Thomas the Tank Engine & Friends™

CREATED BY BRITT ALLCROFT

Based on the Railway Series by the Reverend W Awdry
© 2012 Gullane (Thomas) LLC. A HiT Entertainment company.
Thomas the Tank Engine & Friends and Thomas & Friends are trademarks of Gullane (Thomas) Limited.
Thomas the Tank Engine & Friends and Design is Reg. U.S. Pat. & Tm. Off.

All rights reserved.

ISBN 978 1 4052 6342 9
51521/1
Printed in Italy

HiT entertainment

Welcome to the Thomas Annual 2013! Join Thomas and his friends as they work hard and have lots of fun on the Island of Sodor!

Star in your very own

Thomas & Friends Book!

Thomas

NAME: Thomas

COLOUR: blue with red boiler bands

SIZE: medium

SPEED: average

PERSONALITY: cheeky, friendly

FEATURES: Thomas has 6 small wheels and a yellow 1 on both his sides.

HISTORY: Thomas started off shunting coaches for bigger engines. Later, he was given his own Branch Line and his own carriages, Annie and Clarabel.

Write over Thomas' name.

Thomas

All About Thomas

Thomas was scared when Cranky lifted him high up into the air.

I look ridiculous!

Thomas was not happy when he was fitted with a silly funnel.

Why do you have a moustache, Sir?

Thomas once mixed up The Fat Controller with his brother, Sir Lowham Hatt!

Colour in this picture of Thomas.

Did you know?
Thomas once sent a truck full of books flying when he chuffed along a bumpy track.

Top Ten Engines

Meet the Sodor engines numbered 1 to 10!

Which **engine** do you like best? Write their number here. _____

Percy is **number 6**. He is best friends with Thomas and he loves pulling the mail train.

James is **number 5**. He loves pulling coaches but he hates taking Troublesome Trucks!

Toby is **number 7**. This Steam Tram works on the Quarry Line with his faithful coach, Henrietta.

Duck is **number 8**. His real name is Montague, but everyone calls him Duck because he waddles on his wheels!

Thomas is **number 1**.
He loves taking passengers around Sodor in his carriages, Annie and Clarabel.

Edward is **number 2**.
His Branch Line runs from Brendam Docks to Wellsworth Station.

Gordon is **number 4**.
This big Express Engine is the fastest engine in the Steam Team.

Henry is **number 3**.
He is proud of his green paint and he loves going really fast on the Main Line.

Donald is **number 9**.
He is twins with Douglas. They came from Scotland to join the Steam Team.

Douglas is **number 10**.
The twins were numbered by The Fat Controller when he decided to keep them both.

Sing with Thomas!

Sing along with Thomas and his friends. Shout out the engine numbers and colours!

They're **2**, they're **4**, they're **6**, they're **8**,

shunting trucks and hauling freight,

red and green and brown and blue,

they're the Really Useful crew!

Road, Air or Sea?

Draw lines to show which of Thomas' friends get around Sodor by road, air or sea.

Bertie the Bus

Harold the Helicopter

Captain the Rescue Boat

Sea

Road

Air

Now colour Bertie the Bus bright red.

13

The Best Present of All

Hello, friends!

1 It was a special day on Sodor. Hiro had come back for a holiday.

Let's get a present!

2 "Let's have a welcome party," said Percy. "Let's get a present," said Thomas.

3 Thomas puffed off to look for a present. He would tell everyone about the party too.

14

I'm getting Hiro a present!

4 Thomas told Emily he was getting a present. He forgot to invite her to the party!

5 He told Victor about the present, but he forgot to invite him to the party too!

6 Thomas saw Henry and Gordon too, but he still only talked about the present!

STORY CONTINUED ...

Oh, no!

7 Thomas was chuffing to see Hiro, when he realised. "Oh, no!" he wheeshed. "I haven't told anyone about the party!"

8 Thomas raced around Sodor. He told Emily, Victor, Henry and Gordon about the party. But then he realised he hadn't got a present for Hiro!

9 All the engines were at Hiro's party. Thomas was still sad about not having got a present for Hiro.

Friends are the best present!

10 "But you did get me a present," smiled Hiro. "Having all my friends here is the very best present of all!"

THE END

Rattling Rods!

Salty has to get his rattling rods repaired. Which path leads him to Den at the Dieselworks?

A
B
C

True or False?

1

The lighthouse has red and green stripes.

TRUE   FALSE

2

Thomas is feeling happy.

TRUE   FALSE

How many answers were TRUE?

Thomas is at the beach. Look at the picture then circle the words to say whether each sentence is **TRUE** or **FALSE**.

Here's an example:
Percy is upside-down.

TRUE   FALSE

3

It is a rainy day.

TRUE   FALSE

4

Thomas is pulling an engine.

TRUE   FALSE

5

Thomas has the number 7 on his side.

TRUE   FALSE

How many answers were FALSE?

Make Sir Topham's Hat!

Wear a top hat like The Fat Controller!

You will need:

1 large thick piece of black card

1 large thin piece of black card

1 strip of white paper

a pencil
(ideally white)

child-safe scissors

sticky tape

1 Take a strip of white paper and use it to measure the size of your head. Tape the ends together.

2 Place the paper band on the thick piece of black card. Use a pencil to carefully draw around the inside of the circle.

3 To make the hat brim, draw an outer circle 5cm wide around the smaller circle. Then cut them out as shown.

4 Cut a strip of thin black card 16cm tall. Roll it and tape it to the hat brim, then stick on the top. Now you can wear your top hat just like The Fat Controller!

Did you know?

A long time before The Fat Controller came to the Island of Sodor, a man called The Thin Controller ran the Little Railway, looking after trains like Peter Sam, Sir Handel and Skarloey.

21

cranky

NAME: Cranky

COLOUR: dark green

SIZE: very tall

SPEED: slow

PERSONALITY: grumpy, proud

FEATURES: Cranky has a long, strong crane arm for lifting. He is very tall, so he can see everything that happens at the Docks!

HISTORY: Cranky came to Sodor to help lift heavy loads at Brendam Docks.

Write over Cranky's name.

cranky

All About Cranky

Get me down!

Cranky sometimes tries to sleep without the engines noticing!

YAWN!

Thomas was stuck in the air when Cranky's crane arm broke!

Oooh, this is hard work!

Lifting heavy loads all day can make Cranky extra grumpy!

Colour in this picture of Cranky.

CRANKY

Did you know?

Cranky can be taken apart and moved to other places.

Down at the Docks

1

Cranky the Crane works at the Docks. He lifts and moves heavy things.

Point to Cranky's crates. Can you spot Thomas too?

2

The Docks are where most of Sodor's cargo is loaded and unloaded.

Draw what you want Thomas to deliver here.

You'll find the Docks in Brendam.

3

Ships don't just bring cargo to the Docks. They bring people too!

How many people are waiting for Gordon?

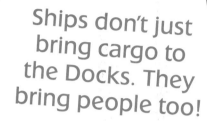

4

Salty works at the Docks because he likes being by the sea.

Salty is missing a colour. Look at the picture above, then finish colouring him in.

Creaky Cranky

It was an **exciting day** on the Island of Sodor. The Duke and Duchess of Boxford were having a spring party! At Brendam Docks, Cranky was busy unloading cargo for the party, when Thomas chuffed onto the dockside.

"It's the Duke and Duchess' party today!" Thomas said happily.

"I don't go to parties," Cranky grumbled loudly. "I'm stuck here."

"You're **creaky**, Cranky! Is everything too heavy for you?" teased Thomas.

But Cranky wasn't in the mood for jokes. "You couldn't pull anything heavy, **tiny Thomas**! That's why Henry and James have the heavy loads today!" Cranky snapped back.

"I'll prove I'm as strong as any other engine!" Thomas told Cranky, and he puffed away to find James. He thought there was more than enough time for him to make his delivery later.

Thomas found James at the Washdown.

"Shall I deliver your wood and barrels to the Docks?" he asked James. "Then you can get ready for the party."

James thought it was a wonderful idea, and soon Thomas was coupled to James' heavy flatbed.

Huffing and puffing, Thomas set off for the Docks.

Thomas **dared** Cranky to try to lift the flatbed. He didn't think the crane would be able to do it. But Cranky did! Thomas was disappointed. He steamed off to find Henry.

Henry was waiting at the coal hopper, so Thomas offered to take his straw bales for him. Henry was delighted.

"Thank you, helpful Thomas!" Henry smiled at him.

Thomas huffed hard to get the straw bales to the Docks, but Cranky managed to lift that flatbed too. This made Thomas really cross!

"Try lifting *me*, Cranky!" Thomas teased the crane.

Cranky didn't want to let Thomas win, so he lowered his hook. But as he lifted Thomas, his crane arm stuttered and **snapped**. Thomas was left hanging in the air!

The Fat Controller arrived at the Docks. "You are causing confusion and delay," he told Thomas. "Cranky is broken, and no deliveries have been made!"

Thomas was very sorry. He knew the delays were all his fault. When the Engineer lowered him onto the track, he set about putting things right. He asked **strong** Spencer to take the wood and straw to the party. Then he set off to collect new parts for Cranky from Victor and Kevin at the Steamworks.

Thomas **rushed** back to the Docks with the heavy parts for Cranky. Cranky was really grateful for Thomas' help.

"Thank you, Thomas," Cranky said. "You're not so *tiny*, after all."

"And you're not *creaky* either," laughed Thomas, as the friends smiled at each other. Thomas decided not to go to the Duke and Duchess' party. He stayed at the Docks so he and Cranky could have their **own party** instead!

THE END

Victor

NAME: Victor

COLOUR: red with yellow boiler bands

SIZE: little

SPEED: average

PERSONALITY: wise, friendly

FEATURES: Victor has hazard stripes on his buffer beams and a lamp above his face, to light his way.

HISTORY: Victor came to Sodor to help manage the Steamworks. He also gave Thomas spare parts to help restore Hiro.

Write over Victor's name.

Victor

All About Victor

Victor wasn't happy when James blew black soot over him!

Humph! This is just great.

ZZZZZZZZ

Victor and Kevin sleep outside the Steamworks after a hard day's work.

Victor sometimes gets cross with Kevin for being clumsy, but they make a good team.

Colour in this picture of Victor.

Did you know?

When Victor went away, Thomas was left in charge of the Steamworks. He didn't do a very good job!

33

Sodor Seaside

1

Read the words, then tick the boxes if you have ever seen the **red** words at the beach.

Edward is passing the **lighthouse** on the way to the beach.

What number is Edward?

2   two

2

The Fat Controller is enjoying an **ice cream** on his day off.

Draw a colourful ice cream on this cone.

3

Ahoy, mateys! Look at all those **seagulls**!

How many seagulls are there on this page?

34

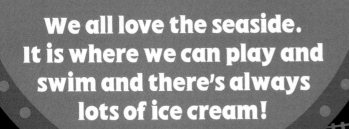

We all love the seaside. It is where we can play and swim and there's always lots of ice cream!

4

There are a lot of **deckchairs** on the beach today.

How many deckchairs can you count?

5

The children are making **sandcastles** with their buckets.

Draw over the sandcastle, then add a flag on the top!

6

Draw here what you would like to do at the beach.

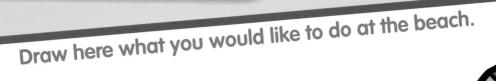

FACT FILE

NAME: Captain

COLOUR: yellow, blue and red, with a white stripe

SIZE: small

SPEED: always quick to the rescue!

PERSONALITY: a quiet hero, calm in any emergency

FEATURES: Captain is a wooden rescue boat with a mast, a lifebelt and an oar.

HISTORY: Captain has his own lifeboat shed at the Search and Rescue Centre. He works there with Rocky and Harold.

I'm always ready to rescue anyone in need of help.

Draw over the dotted lines to finish me off.

Captain is part of the Sodor Search and Rescue Team. He is very brave and always in control in emergency situations.

Colour in Captain's face. Don't forget his big bushy eyebrows!

Kevin and Victor Maze

Kevin's late for a job at the Steamworks. Help him get through the maze to Victor as quickly as possible.

Spot the Difference

Can you spot the 6 differences in the second picture of Thomas and The Fat Controller?

Make Jeremy the Jet

Make your very own jet plane!

You will need:

1 plastic yoghurt or dessert pot

1 large card tube

1 small card tube

glue

child-safe scissors

white, blue and black paints

paintbrushes

thick white card

1 Draw these shapes on the thick card and cut them out. Carefully cut two slits where the red dotted lines appear. The lengths shown are for guidance only.

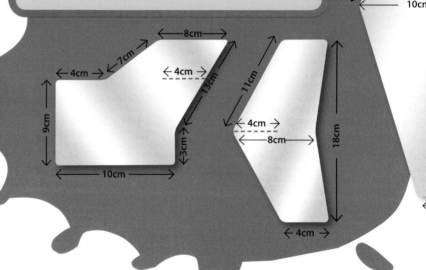

20cm
10cm
38cm
5cm
8cm
7cm
4cm
4cm
13cm
11cm
9cm
3cm
4cm
8cm
18cm
10cm
4cm

2 Glue the dessert pot to the large tube and paint both white. When dry, cut 3 big slits in the tube as shown. Then paint the small tube white and when it is dry, cut it in half.

10cm
15cm
15cm

ASK A
GROWN-UP
TO HELP YOU!

3 To slot the pieces together, Insert the cut-out wing into the 2 largest slits on either side of the tube.

Slot the tail fin into the top of the tail.

Then insert the cut-out tail into the smaller slit as shown.

4 Glue the 2 halves of the small tube onto the sides of the body. Paint on the blue markings as shown, then draw on Jeremy's eyes and windows. Then add a big smile.

Now Jeremy's ready for take-off!

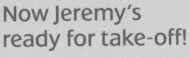

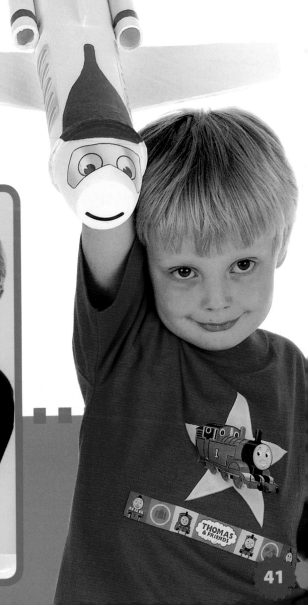

Hiro

NAME: Hiro

COLOUR: black with gold bands and red wheels

SIZE: large

SPEED: average

PERSONALITY: wise, kind, friendly

FEATURES: Hiro has a lamp, his name on a gold plate and the number 51 on his tender.

HISTORY: Hiro is a very old engine. He was forgotten until Thomas found him and helped to get him restored!

Write over Hiro's name.

Hiro

All About Hiro!

QUACK! QUACK! QUACK!

I don't like looking scruffy!

Percy and Hiro like to relax with the ducks by the lake.

When Thomas found Hiro, he was very rusty and dirty. Even his lamp was broken!

Sorry, Sir!

Hiro was red-faced when he made The Fat Controller cross for not being Really Useful.

Colour in this picture of Hiro.

Did you know?

Hiro was the first steam engine to arrive on Sodor.

Hiro

Helps Out

Enjoy this story about Hiro, who helps everyone out!

1 One day, as he puffed into Knapford, Hiro saw that The Fat Controller was missing his hat!

2 He looked very worried. "Oh dear! What a busy day. Where is my hat?" he said.

3 Edward puffed up. "The Fat Controller is worried about his busy day," Hiro said.

4 The Fat Controller returned with his hat. "I have a meeting about the railway," he said and quickly left.

5

Edward was worried. "I haven't been told where to take my passengers," he wheeshed.

6

Hiro told him to go to the hills. He liked being Master of the Railway.

7

Later, Hiro met Thomas. He was going to ask The Fat Controller where to take his trucks.

8

"The Fat Controller is very busy," said Hiro. "Wait until later." Hiro enjoyed helping The Fat Controller.

9 QUACK, QUACK!

Then Hiro met Percy. He was going to ask The Fat Controller where to take his load of ducks.

10

"The Fat Controller is very busy," Hiro said. "It will have to wait."

11 Then Hiro met The Fat Controller. He was very cross. "None of my engines have done their jobs!" he boomed.

12 Hiro felt terrible. He thought he was helping. "I'm sorry, Sir," he said. "I'll fix this mess right away!"

13 Hiro found Edward in the hills. He sent him to Knapford to see The Fat Controller.

14 He found Thomas by the farm and then wheeshed off to find Percy too.

15 Hiro puffed into Knapford. All the engines had left to do their jobs. "What should I do?" he asked The Fat Controller nervously.

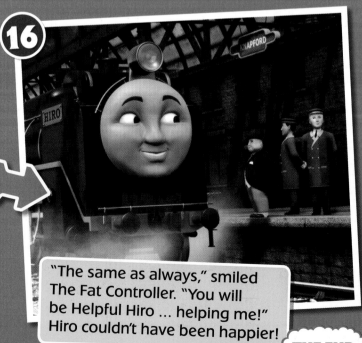

16 "The same as always," smiled The Fat Controller. "You will be Helpful Hiro … helping me!" Hiro couldn't have been happier!

THE END

Really Useful Thomas!

The Fat Controller gives a special card to engines who are Really Useful. Thomas has impressed him today, so colour in Thomas to complete his card!

REALLY USEFUL

4 Where is Toby?

5 How many engines are there altogether?

6 Which engine do you like best?

Answers: 1. 3; 2. Emily is the third engine from the right; 3. 3; 4. Toby is on the right; 5. There are 8 engines altogether.

Whiff

NAME: Whiff

COLOUR: dark green with black lining

SIZE: average

SPEED: slow

PERSONALITY: friendly, cheerful

FEATURES: Whiff is the only engine on Sodor who wears glasses. He also looks a little grubby most of the time!

HISTORY: Whiff came to Sodor to help collect the rubbish. He loves his job!

Write over Whiff's name.

Whiff

All About Whiff!

Whiff is really helpful. He helps The Fat Controller whether it's day or night.

Emily tries to avoid smelly Whiff at first. He has to search all over Sodor to find her!

Time to collect more rubbish!

Whiff loves collecting dirty rubbish. He has a look and smell all of his own!

Colour in this picture of Whiff.

Did you know?

Daisy thought Whiff's rubbish always smelled bad until he collected some freshly cut grass.

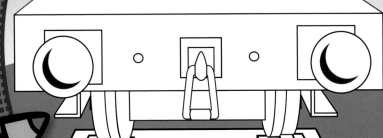

51

...ark

What colours are the stripes on the wall? Can you think of an animal with the same stripes?

What animal has Thomas delivered to the Animal Park?

giraffe

Gordon got a fright when he heard the animals in the Animal Park for the first time!

Make Engine Cakes!

Ask a grown-up to help you make these delicious cupcakes, then decorate them with engine faces and numbers!

1 A grown-up will need to preheat the oven to 200°C, 400°F, Gas Mark 6 and line a muffin tin with 12 cake cases.

You will need:

- 125g self-raising flour
- 125g caster sugar
- 125g soft unsalted butter
- 2 eggs
- ½ tsp vanilla extract
- 2 tbsp milk
- icing sugar
- white fondant icing
- pre-coloured fondant icing
- jam or honey
- black icing pen or liquorice

2 Put all the ingredients (except for the milk) in a food processor and whizz until smooth. If you don't have a processor, cream the butter and sugar together with a wooden spoon, beat in the eggs one at time, adding the flour gradually and finally add the vanilla extract.

3 Then add the milk a little at a time, until the mixture drops easily off a spoon.

4 Use the spoon to divide the cake mixture evenly between the 12 cake cases.

5 Ask a grown-up to put the muffin tin in the preheated oven to bake for 15-20 minutes, or until they are golden brown and firm to the touch.

6 Cool them in their paper cases on a wire rack.

7

Once the cakes are cool, you can decorate them! Pre-coloured fondant icing is available in a variety of colours, including black. The black can be mixed with white fondant to create the grey engine faces.

8

Cover a surface with a light dusting of icing sugar. Roll out the icing and ask an adult to use a sharp knife to cut out the shapes you need. A drop of honey or jam will stick your icing onto the cakes. You can buy a black icing pen to add the details of the faces, or use strips of black liquorice cut to size.

SAFETY NOTE: Always ask a grown-up to help when using hot ovens, kitchen appliances and sharp knives.

Gordon

NAME: Gordon

COLOUR: blue, with red and yellow lining

SIZE: big

SPEED: fast

PERSONALITY: proud, big-headed

FEATURES: Gordon is the strongest engine on Sodor. He pulls the passenger Express train.

HISTORY: Gordon has pulled the Queen's royal train, and visited London. Before he arrived on Sodor, he was painted dark green.

Write over Gordon's name.

Gordon

Gordon Facts!

Gordon came to a sudden stop when a tree fell on the track!

Gordon got a shock when a huge snowball rolled down the line!

Brrr, this is going to be chilly!

It's just not fair!

Gordon wasn't happy when Edward was given a more important job than him!

Colour in this picture of Gordon.

Did you know?

Gordon hates pulling goods trucks so much, he runs into ditches and stops on hills on purpose!

57

SEARCH & RESCUE

Who is on the turntable?

The Sodor Search and Rescue Centre is opening. All of the engines have come to celebrate!

SODOR SEARCH AND RESCUE

Can you see Toby the Tram Engine on the tracks?

Point to Captain the Life Boat.

CAN YOU FIND THESE THINGS IN THE BIG PICTURE?

COLOUR IN A BALLOON WHEN YOU FIND THEM.

Make The Fat Controller

Make your very own Sir Topham Hatt!

You will need:

- 1 large egg
- glue
- black felt-tip pen
- 1 small cardboard tube
- child-safe scissors
- sticky tape
- a pin
- some paper

Glue

1 Take a large egg and, using a pin, make a hole at both ends. Now gently blow into one hole so the insides blow out of the other hole into a bowl. Use a black felt-tip pen to draw The Fat Controller's face on the egg.

2 Photocopy The Fat Controller's clothes and stick them around the cardboard tube as shown.

3 To make his hat, photocopy his hat pieces and cut them out.

4 Stick the pieces of his hat together and put it on his head. Doesn't he look **splendid!**

Glue

ASK A GROWN-UP TO HELP YOU!

All About The Fat Controller

Sir Topham Hatt, or The Fat Controller, came to Sodor as a Railway Engineer and later became the Director of the Railway. He became a 'Sir' when he was awarded a knighthood for his services to the railway industry!

Rocky

NAME: Rocky

COLOUR: burgundy with yellow hazard stripes

SIZE: large

SPEED: other engines have to pull him!

PERSONALITY: a gentle giant, everyone's best friend

FEATURES: Rocky does all the heavy lifting with his rotating crane arm.

HISTORY: Rocky is an important part of the Sodor Search and Rescue Team. He always comes to the rescue!

Join the dots to draw around Rocky's steam.

I'm always on hand to clear up a mess!

Rocky works with the Search and Rescue Team. He is very strong and he can lift engines who have broken down or had an accident.

Gordon's Shortcut

This is a story about when Gordon learnt a lesson about shortcuts.

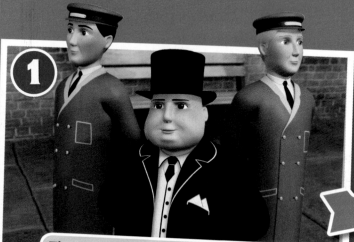

1 The Fat Controller was waiting with the guards at Knapford Station.

2 Gordon was waiting too. He had to take Stanley's passengers to Brendam Docks but Stanley was la

3 You're late!

Puff! Puff! Stanley finally chugged in. "Sorry, I took a shortcut and got lost!" he said.

4 When the passengers were aboard Gordon, The Fat Controller said he had another job for the engines to do.

5 "I should pick up the VIPs!"

"I need two engines to pick up some Very Important Passengers and some workmen from Great Waterton," he explained.

6

Gordon wanted to collect the VIPs, but first he had to go to Brendam Docks.

7

Afterwards, he rushed off to Great Waterton. "I'll take a shortcut under the bridge," he puffed. "I never get lost!"

8 "Are you lost, Gordon?"

But when he steamed through, he saw Ben, not Great Waterton Station.

9 "I'm too busy to talk!"

Gordon was worried. Stanley might reach Great Waterton before him now. He whizzed past Ben.

10 "I am too important to pick up workmen!"

"I must get there first. I don't want to be the engine collecting the workmen!" he thought.

11

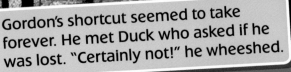

Gordon's shortcut seemed to take forever. He met Duck who asked if he was lost. "Certainly not!" he wheeshed.

12

Help!

Then he puffed up to a junction and didn't recognise where he was. "Now I really am lost!"

13

Then he spotted Stanley far ahead of him. There were logs on the line and he was stuck!

14

Gordon knew his shortcut hadn't worked and now he needed to find help for Stanley. "Please stop!" he cried, as Harvey passed by.

15

Harvey was happy to help clear the logs off the line.

16

Soon Gordon and Stanley arrived at Great Waterton together. "No more shortcuts for me!" laughed Gordon.

THE END

Tip Top Colouring

The Fat Controller needs a hat.
Draw one on his head, then colour it in!

The Fat Controller loves trains that run on time.

He doesn't like trains who are too big for their buffers!

His real name is Sir Topham Hatt!

67

Thomas' Special Delivery

Help Thomas deliver a new hat to The Fat Controller. But watch out for fallen trees on the track!

Answer: Thomas needs to take the track across the top and down the right side of the maze to get to The Fat Controller.